The Summer of Strawberry Rhubarb Pie

A Collection of Stories and Poems from the Heart

Jane Herr Desrosiers

Fulton Books
Meadville, PA

Published by Fulton Books 2023

ISBN 979-8-88731-239-2 (paperback)
ISBN 979-8-88731-240-8 (digital)

Printed in the United States of America

Contents

Introduction

The Summer of Strawberry Rhubarb Pie reminds us of the seasons of our life and the way that we adapt to them. My life has been filled with an array of people and a roller coaster of experiences throughout my seasons.

Through these stories and poems, fictional and nonfictional, you will hopefully imagine some of yourself in these reflections of life. We as humans find a way to adapt, laugh, or cry at our circumstances, and for better or worse, move on. And perhaps, enjoy a slice of pie along the way.

The Summer of Strawberry Rhubarb Pie

Part I

I parted leaves the size of an elephant's ear, finding the red-and-green-hued stalk, and gave a gentle tug. It pulled away from the crown of the plant a huge leaf and fanned myself, as Cleopatra might have been cooled by her servants. I continued to pull several more stalks. I only needed two cups of fruit for my strawberry rhubarb pie. With the rest, I would make rhubarb sauce. With a quick *thwack* from my sharp knife, I lopped off the leaves and the ends.

My strawberry bed, even though it was June, wouldn't hold enough berries for a pie. I would have to make do with the store-bought ones. While they were large and bright red, their taste paled by comparison to the ones that were slowly ripening in my backyard garden. When I was back inside, I washed the rhubarb and the strawberries and began to chop.

My husband, Joe, walked into the kitchen and asked, "Who died?"

"You remember Paul Simms? His sister passed last week. Poor thing. She had cancer just about everywhere when she finally went to the doctor. Anyway, the service is this afternoon," I replied.

"Why don't you make something easy like brownies?" he said and grabbed a blueberry muffin that I'd baked this morning using the frozen berries from last year's crop.

"Because doing this gives me time to think about the person. The ones who have passed and the ones who are left. If I made something quick, I wouldn't have time to let my mind remember them and why they're in my life. And when you eat a piece of pie, it takes you a little longer than if it was a two-bite brownie. Pie allows you to take a moment and maybe share that moment with someone." I finished the chopping, dropped the diced fruit into the sugar and tapioca mix, added some fresh orange zest, a bit of cinnamon and stirred. The pie dough was waiting to transform this fragrant mix into a ten-inch circle of golden crust filled sweetness.

"Ah the writer in you can always bring those visions to life, and that's why I love you," he said as he kissed me on the cheek, took another muffin, and headed out the door. "I'm late shift today. I should be home by six." Joe worked as a salesman/mechanic at Lewis' Farm Equipment and Supply store. He'd been there since he came back from his stint with the Marines. He'd been in the Persian Gulf war and had hung around for the beginning of Afghanistan and thankfully came home unscathed.

I spooned the filling into the pie crust. For the top crust, I took one of my small cookie cutters and cut out three tiny flowers in the center. I folded the crust in half and gently laid it on top of the bright red-and-green mixture. The orange zest and the cinnamon delivered an infusion that was fruity and fresh into the air. Laying the crust on and pinching the two layers together, it was almost done. Finally, I took a beaten egg, added some water, and started to paint the top. The egg and water mixture would leave a shiny crust.

Footsteps coming up onto the porch stairs signaled that Maddie was back from feeding the chickens.

"Mama, who's the pie for?" she asked. She set a basket filled with more than a dozen eggs on the counter. She washed her hands and then took the brush from my hand and finished the rest of the paint job. I stepped aside and started to make an aluminum foil collar for the crust. Maddie sprinkled the shiny wet top with a generous amount of sugar.

"Paul Simms. His sister Celia passed. The service is this afternoon." I finished the collar and took the pie from Maddie, placed the foil around the edges, and slid the pie into the oven.

"No! She was the nicest woman. She sure could belt out those hymns." Maddie was sixteen but wise beyond her years.

Joe and I adopted Maddie after I'd lost my second baby. Maddie's parents, Alice and Robert, were killed in a car accident. They were celebrating his promotion that night in Smithville. Robert missed the corner by Bowen's Bridge, and the car sunk in the cold waters of the Platen River. Maddie had been home with a babysitter. There weren't any relatives close by, so as longtime members of church, we offered to take care of her until things got settled. Maddie was four at the time, and our Jonathan was six, so they each found a new friend and playmate.

As it turned out, Alice's sister, Elaine, had no interest in taking on a four-year-old. She was ten years older than Alice and told us she wasn't equipped, as she put it, to raise a child. Robert's brother Henry had four kids of his own and lived out in Montana and didn't think he'd be able to feed and clothe one more child. During the days before the funerals, we quickly realized that Maddie had no real connection with her aunt or her uncle. And it was also obvious that both of them were only really interested in whatever assets Maddie's parents had left. Outside the house and their car, which had been totaled in the accident, there was little else other than the contents of the house. In their will, Maddie's parents had assigned the care of her over to Elaine or Henry along with the contents of the home.

Seeing their lack of interest in Maddie herself, we approached them about our adopting Maddie, and it didn't take long for them to decide. They signed papers for us to adopt Maddie, divided up the contents between the themselves, let us take what we needed for her, and then had a sale for the rest. The house was a small cape, and it went up on the market within the month. It sold a few months later. Joe and I waited for a possible portion of the sale to help with Maddie, but as we had guessed early on, nothing came.

Before she left town with her half of the remnants of her sister's life, Elaine paid us a visit. She told us that in their will, Maddie's parents had listed a $50,000 life insurance policy that named Maddie as the beneficiary. That money would be hers when she turned twenty-one. She'd found the policy in a desk drawer and upon examining document, it did indeed name Maddie as the sole beneficiary on her twenty-first birthday. Elaine begrudgingly handed the policy over to Joe and I and said, "Good luck with her. God knows I couldn't handle a four-year old." After she left, I was most certain that God did know exactly where Maddie belonged.

"Mama, can I go with you?" Maddie asked. "I'd like to give Mr. Simms a big hug."

"Why, of course you can. It'll be nice to have some company." I smiled at my girl.

"Too bad Jon's working. He liked her too. She used to give him cookies when he shoveled her sidewalk." She started to pile the bowls into the sink to wash.

"I know he would. But Tucker's got to get their produce picked and down to the farm market for tomorrow's big summer event. We won't see him until after dark." Jon had worked at Tucker's Farm after school and summers since he was twelve. They were one of the largest farms in the valley. From asters to zucchinis, Tucker's was well known. And now that Jon was eighteen and waiting on making his next life decision, he was in charge of coordinating deliveries to the market and setting up.

"I'm going upstairs to take a shower and get dressed. Unless you need me to do anything else?" Her hand was already on the stair rail that led to the back of our second floor.

"No, all set. Thank you for asking. You go on and get ready. I'll finish up here."

I went out to the back porch to sit for a bit and read my book. The pie would have another forty minutes or so before it was done— enough time for me to get back into the book. I was a member of the town library's book club and I only had one more week to finish this month's selection. It was about the struggles of a pioneer family, and while the characters were likable, it seemed to me that the author had lifted them from a TV series from the seventies.

"Your books are much better than that." The comment came from my dear friend and neighbor, Liz. Liz was also in the book club and was never hesitant to voice her opinion on most things. She'd walked through the neighbor gate of the hedgerow and now took a seat on the porch swing.

"Don't I know it. Are you finished with it?" I asked, thankful to put the book down.

"I used my Evelyn Wood skills and ramrodded my way through this sorry excuse of literary excellence." She screwed up her nose to let me know she was not a fan of this particular author.

"Lucky you. Maybe there's a CliffsNotes version, so I don't have to endure the rest of this?" I inquired.

"I'd rather doubt that there's anything written about this one. Seems like it would be on the fifty-cent table at the TownMart Bargain Book section." We both chuckled at that. "Seriously though, what are you working on now?"

"I'm working on two new books, but I lost some momentum since Jackie passed," I replied. I had published a cozy mystery series of five books over the past eight years, and these were doing well. My publisher had asked for more, but the ideas weren't flowing. With my sister, Jackie, ill for the past two years, my attentions had been more helping to care for her than most things in my own home.

"How callous of me, of course," Liz said.

"No worries, it is what it is. We're all going to go sometime, but when it's family, it just seems that you never want that time to be here," I answered. "You going to the funeral for Celia?" I asked. "I'm making a pie."

"I am. I filled some rolls with ham salad," Liz replied.

"You can come with Maddie and me, if you'd like," I offered. "Service is at noon."

"Thanks, I'd like that. I'll be back at eleven," she said and she jumped off the side of the porch and disappeared through the hedgerow.

*****

After the church service, we all gathered under the maple trees at the back of the church grounds. Tables had been set up with white flowy tablecloths. The metal chairs were filling in as everyone filed out of church. Liz and I were helping the Ladies Auxiliary set out the food and serve some plates to the elderly folks.

Maddie had gone over to speak to Paul. I saw her give him a hug and a handshake. She told me that she could still remember the day of her parents' funeral. Most people had passed her by thinking that because she was only four, she wouldn't understand or that she'd forget. Now, she would always ask to go with me to a funeral service and made it a point to speak to anyone who had been affected by the death. As I said, she truly was wise beyond her years.

Looking around, I saw the two of them sitting at the end of the table: Blanche and Millie. They'd been friends for more than seventy years. They were dressed in light blouses and summer skirts. Blanche, with her still brown wavy hair, worn in the same style that she'd had ever since I'd known her. And Millie looked like she'd been to the hairdressers that morning. Or so I overheard her daughter-in-law, Lilly, tell Judy Simms about Millie's weekly trip. And that next January would be Millie's one hundredth birthday. Blanche was the younger of the two, at ninety-six years old.

I cut two pieces of my strawberry rhubarb pie and brought them over to their table.

"How would you ladies like a piece of my pie?" I asked as I set the paper plates and forks on the table.

"You won't need to ask twice, Sally, this looks scrumptious. Thank you," Blanche remarked and pulled a plate toward her.

"Well, if she's having one, I guess I will too." Millie looked up at me with her smile. "Why don't you sit with us for a while? We haven't talked to you for a long time."

"I'd love to," I said and I pulled out a folding chair and sat down. The metal felt cool through my cotton shift. The heat of early June was in full force today, and the coolness of the chair was welcome.

"How are you two getting along? You look wonderful," I said, and they both beamed. Being the elder ladies of the town, they took pride in their longevity and independence.

"They took the keys to my Buick away last fall. Don't know if you heard about that," Millie admitted and shook her head in disgust.

"But now you have a chauffeur. Lilly will take you anywhere you want," Blanche said and tried to shine a positive light on it.

"I guess, but I don't like the way she drives. Too fast for my taste," she replied and took another bite of pie. "This is very tasty. Your mom taught you well."

"Why thanks. I keep trying her various crust recipes. She had different ones for different fillings. Some turn out better than others." My mom had been the consummate baker with yeast breads and pies and everything in between.

"Don't be so hard on yourself, Sally," Blanche added. "The world will do that for you. Don't give it any extra help." We laughed at that comment. "You know we could use your soprano voice back at church." She watched for my reaction after those words.

"I know, Blanche. But Joe doesn't like the way Howard delivers the message. Says he's just reading from some mail-order sermon. He liked it when Al was here," I said.

"Al did appeal to the men, what with his sports references. And he knew his stuff. I'd bring my Bible along and look up everything he was saying. He was always right on the money," Blanche remarked.

"I'm waiting for a female minister to come into town," Millie said with a slight sniff. "Until then, Blanche comes to visit me after service each Sunday. We sit and have coffee and read the paper. That reminds me, I need to have Lilly pick up some more Sanka."

"Promise me that you'll make two of these pies when I die. And don't forget the song," Blanche said in between mouthfuls of my pie.

"Blanche, you're not going anywhere," Millie said. "Besides, I think I got my ticket before yours. And what do you mean *your song*?"

"Oh, when Sally was in the folk group at church, she found a funny little ditty about the cemetery for the stars out in Hollywood. You have to promise me." Blanche looked straight into my eyes, and there was nothing that I could do but answer in the affirmative.

"Even if I can't play my guitar any more, I promise you that I'll sing it." I took in a small sigh and thought of a world without Blanche or Milly. They were the history of our town; there wasn't anything that I could ask them that they didn't know or, for that matter, had been a part of.

People come and go in your life; that was certain. Whether or not you wanted them to, they just did. And it seems that the ones you wanted to keep were always out of your grasp. A fingertip closer, and you could hold onto them forever. But for now, I looked across the table at these two old gals, talking and kidding each other like they'd done for more years than most people were given the time to be here. They knew their time was nearing its end, but they lived and laughed and were more alive than some people half their ages. And that was a good way to be.

Weeding

<pre>
The seedlings are up
Carrots
Beets
The weeds are up too
Unarmed
All look like fine green hair
All must be weeded
My tiny fingers act like combs that will pluck the weeds
Go too fast and more seedlings than weeds will come out
Then Daddy will be mad
Go too slow
Daddy is still mad that you are slow
The soil is warm on my toes
My feet are dirty all summer
</pre>

Growing Vegetables

I love growing vegetables. Every spring, I eagerly bring just enough tender green plants home to begin the annual nurturing. Water, fertilizer, pinch, stake—all to a bountiful end. Today there were two tomato plants, a pickling cucumber, two peppers, and an assortment of herbs waiting for the daily watering. The fuzzy leaves of the cucumber parted like a curtain going up on a performance to find the day's vegetable star. Only two cucumbers were center stage. Twisting their spiny stems, I picked both of them. I brought them back to the kitchen where they joined the dozen or so others of their kind who were awaiting their fate on my counter.

I reminisced back to the garden at my parent's home when we would pick pecks and bushels of vegetables, our garden taking up about a quarter of an acre. The pickling and canning process would begin within moments of picking. The likes of a cucumber dill sauce that would be served over grilled salmon, or a wonderful garlicky Greek tzatziki sauce made of pureed cucumbers were not the options in the fifties. We made pickles. Lots and lots of pickles. Blue enamel roasting pans held thin slices of cucumbers and onions, soaking in their sweet briny baths. Those were for the bread and butter pickles. Bottles were sterilized, then filled, capped, and positioned in the wire basket. Steam rose from the boiling water in the blue enamel pots that would seal in the freshness.

Dill pickles were a subterranean process. Our stone cellar held several large gray earthenware crocks where the cucumbers were brined with garlic, vinegar, salt, water, and loads of fresh dill. They were covered with a glass pie plate, a clean linen cloth, and a rock. This kept them protected and submerged in their brine. Once covered, the crock was set in place, and we were not to peek until at least two weeks passed. Time was all we had back then. When you finally held those fat juicy pickles and tasted that deep garlic and dill flavor, the juice running down your hand into your wrist and the sleeve of your shirt, you knew the wait had been worth it. As the weeks went by, the flavor and colors changed until the bright green of half sours aged into the deeper yellow green color, signaling a fully dilled pickle.

But none of that laborious process for me today. Being a woman of technology, I searched online for something different to make. There were thousands of choices from cucumber soup, fried cucumbers, to Asian fusion cucumber chicken. Not satisfied with anything there, I next tried some of the many cookbooks in my collection. While there were a couple of maybes, nothing hit me. I finally reached up to my top shelf and brought down the faded blue wooden recipe box. My fingers picked through the many dog-eared cards that stuffed the box. Finding the recipe, I withdrew the worn card that my friend, Cheryl, had given me so very long ago and prepared my ingredients. Yes, after all the endless culinary possibilities, I was making pickles.

Was it a bit of nostalgia that had hit me as I roamed through the pages of my cookbooks? Some had been my mother's, with page corners turned over to mark the best ones. Those moments of her pickling prowess: her faded blue apron fastened to her sturdy frame making the perfect pickle for her family; today I wanted to go back to the beginning. Well, almost.

Although my pickles would use the refrigerator to speed their process from fresh cucumbers to pickled delights, the taste was the same. In no time the brine was made, the cucumbers were sliced, and into the refrigerator they went. The flavor memories of the simple bread and butter pickle brought me instantly back to Sunday dinner. There would be a salty fat-crusted pork roast accompanied by creamy mashed potatoes and silken brown gravy. Add to that the sweet tart snap of the pickles, and there was nothing better.

Years earlier, after a meal, my sisters, my mom, and I set about our task of cleaning up. If you were lucky enough to be in charge of leftovers, you were assured the last lick of the spoon of mashed potatoes where you stole a dip into that delicious gravy. The kitchen was where the conversations of life took place. Whether it was about school, or work, or the neighbors, dishes were never done in silence. Nowadays, the dishwasher is filled, buttons are pushed, and people scatter to pursue their interests. Such a shame. Time saved, but not shared.

It seems that all the things we do and have today are made to help us create more time in our busy lives. But time for what? Back then, when we had free time, we would go visiting. Not a text, a tweet, or an invite on Facebook or an email. But a face-to-face, sit-down under the maple tree on a metal swing or broad-armed wooden chairs, honest-to-goodness "How are things going today?" visiting. Oh, I'm a culprit of all the trappings of modern-day technology. Don't think I'm not. However, if you get the chance to have a fond memory come back to you, indulge yourself. Your mind has just given you a chance to return to that moment. Sit back and enjoy it.

Coveting Thy Special Cookie

They're on sale! What's on sale, you ask? I'm talking about the famous chocolate sandwich cookie with the creamy white filling. Oreo! Oh, boy! Now, which ones to choose? There seems to be more varieties every time I'm in the grocery store. I put several packages in my cart. Thin ones, double stuffed, and mint; some would go home with me, and others would go off to my grandkids.

Showing your grandchildren the correct way to dunk their cookies in milk is in the grandparents' manual of *Things to Teach Your Grandchildren*. Big plus: it allows you to put your diet aside for a moment and indulge in at least one or two cookies. If only buying them had been this easy when I was young.

Growing up, my life in the 1950s was darn good. We lived in the country, and in today's jargon, we were a farm-to-table family. My dad worked swing shifts in a mill and my mom was a telephone operator for Ma Bell. So that meant that the farm-to-table part of life was after work and on weekends, with as much child labor as they could get out of my sisters and myself.

My father loved to hunt and fish, so there was always the seasonal catch of the moment. From succulent roasts of venison, pheasant, or duck, and ending with crispy fried trout and cod, our protein layer in the food triangle was well taken care of. And my mother was a culinary whiz at cooking, canning, freezing, and pickling fruits and vegetables. I still remember having peaches in February that we had frozen the summer before. In their simple syrup, there was nothing that compared to those sweet meaty orangey yellow crescents. My mom was also a consummate baker, churning out pies, cakes, and yeast rolls. It was like magic, watching her take flour, sugar, and eggs and transforming them into delicious treats.

But there was always that one thing that my mom could not recreate. The chocolate sandwich cookie. Two crisp chocolate wafers that captured a sweet and creamy white filling between them. Not whoopie pies. But no, the best milk dunking cookies ever made. However, there were two national brands that competed for our loyalty. While they each claimed to be the best, there was a noticeable difference between the two. One seemed to have more of the creamy filling, while the other had a crispier cookie. In the end, cost was the primary reason for choosing one over the other. This only made the higher-priced cookie that much more prestigious than the other in our house.

A package of prime chocolate delights was purchased every once in a while and then kept for special occasions or as a reward. As a nine-year-old, this was a veritable heartache. I could only have the other brand of cookies in my lunch box. Surely, hadn't I had been a good child? I had finished my supper without too much coaxing. Wasn't that special? Couldn't that coveted package be opened and savored? "No, not today" was always the answer.

What eventually ended up happening, as you might be able to surmise, the coveted confections were stale when the package was finally opened. This was cause for all types of excuses of why we should have opened them earlier, or maybe they just weren't that good. Not that good? Who was my mom trying to kid? Those were the best cookies ever!

Keeping the best for a special occasion was a mantra that my family and most families of our generation subscribed to. There were always the clothes that were kept and labeled for church, or your school shoes, or your good coat. The problem with that was, as a growing child, well, I grew. And by the time that special occasion came around again, most things were too small. I still have pictures of myself on Easter Sunday; one year apart, with my Sunday coat too big one year and the next it showed too small. Excuses abounded and ranged from my eating too much and ended with the fact that we must have bought the wrong size to begin with. Mom and Dad always had varying opinions about me. My mom defended my growing girl spurts. Shopping trips to Hartford or Providence were sure to solve any wardrobe issues. While my dad, it seemed, carried that lingering disappointment that I hadn't born a boy. Being the oops baby (term used when there was eleven years between the last child born and your birth!), I'm sure my father had wished with all his might for a boy. There would have been no need for an Easter hat and coat if my name had been John.

My father passed away in his early eighties. My mother followed along some ten years later. When we began to clean up our old family home, I was dismayed at what we found. Packages of unopened soft pastel percale sheets, so different from the thin white muslin ones that had always been "good enough" on their bed. Gift boxes of fluffy towel sets that would have felt luxurious and softened the ravages that their illnesses had left behind. Pretty clothes with tags hanging from the sleeves, waiting at the ready for that special day. Glassware and dishes in unopened boxes had waited to hold that special food on that special occasion that never came.

My sisters and I shared the favorite things, plates and bowls and our grandmother's best China, among ourselves. It gave us reminders of the hands that had touched them. And those special days when they had been filled with the wonderful food of our Polish/German heritage.

As I look back on the way that my parents lived and brought us up, I understand the need to have restraint in how we live our lives. Pennies pinched and buying only what you need instead of what you want. That's basic. But I bet everyone who is reading this has that special something that they are waiting to use or eat or wear. Every day, in some small way, should be special for you and those around you. So my advice: use the pretty dish for your popcorn. Wear that new shirt to the grocery store before it goes out of style, or heaven forbid, it no longer fits. And, oh yes, eat the damn special cookie. You'll be amazed at how satisfied and special you'll feel.

Sewing and Other Domestic Adventures

When I was working, I took Mondays off during the summer. I liked being off on Mondays. No pressure to prepare for the coming events of the weekend if I had taken Friday off. Just a day to chill out, get caught up, and get ready to go back to work.

One such Monday, I did a number of things that were these catch-up items. Some of those things I did that day brought back a flood of memories from my childhood. I had grown up in the country, although not that different from where I live now. While it hadn't been a farm with all the requisite array of animals and red tractors and barns, my home and my family taught me many things.

I was up early before seven, had coffee, and read the two newspapers. Two newspapers were essential as my husband is a sports enthusiast. And our local paper never had quite enough information about the scores from the games played the day before. Hence, his need for the one published in the city. And I required the local paper for the obituaries. I'm nosy, but I'm also at the age when my cohorts could be facing an early departure. Once I was assured that everyone I knew or had heard of was still with us, I set about to straighten things up. One trip upstairs brought me by my husband's office. He was out of town for the day, and I almost walked by when I noticed the piece of fabric that I had purchased a few months ago. I had promised to make him new curtains.

Seizing the day, or rather the fabric, I took it to my bedroom and, using my bed as my cutting board, started to cut and measure. There was just enough to make the two valances needed. As I stood at my ironing board, I thanked the inventor of iron on interfacing. A simple turn and a hot iron fused the material together. Growing up, our sewing projects had many rules and little conveniences. Edges had to be turned and sewn and then hemmed. I think it was just a ploy from the thread companies to make us use more thread for our sewing assignments.

With only one edge to be sewn on each valance, I headed downstairs to my sewing machine. While I don't suggest everyone have a machine in their living room, I do advocate for one where you have natural light. That is, if you can sew at all. I opened the machine, plugged it in, and arranged my foot pedal. I slid the window open and welcomed the warm morning breeze. I could smell the fresh mown grass and I could hear the cows bellowing at a nearby farm. It was a very idyllic setting, one I'm sure that Norman Rockwell could have painted.

Memories came back as I threaded the machine. Although most people would never think about it, a sewing machine has a specific path that the thread must follow on the machine to produce a stitch. And while I could probably do it with my eyes closed, I remembered back to when my mother would stand over me, time and time again, to make sure it was done right. Our sewing machine had been in the dining room in front of a window. When I had a project, my vigilant mother would wear out a path from the kitchen to the dining room to make sure I was following the directions and sewing a straight seam line.

The knowledge of sewing and all sorts of things were passed from my mother to my sisters and me. Most of these life lessons centered around the basics of cooking and maintaining a home. But there were other things that, while not necessarily taught, were the examples of how to live your life. For instance, take the squishing of a bug that was about to devour a plant's blossom. You learned that you would live if you touched a bug, but you learned not to be afraid of new things.

My mother also passed along her love of reading maps and, more importantly, folding them. When a friend or a family member was on vacation, we would rummage through her collection of maps to see just where they were. The information brought with it a yearning for independent travel and led to our many road trips across New England, my mother at the wheel and me with the map in my hands. This gave me a sense of direction in all aspects of my world as I headed out of the comforts of home.

When you have the ability and the knowledge to accomplish any number of tasks or projects, you may tend to develop a level of impatience with those who are not in possession of that same knowledge. This trait did not miss being passed along to me. My mother was a bit more patient with me than I am of, well, anyone. Learning to take a breath, articulate instructions, and wait is a mantra I say almost every day.

I wonder what types of information gets passed down to the next generation these days. I do know my daughter always asks me why I know how to do so many random things. I smile and explain that things were different when I grew up and that we had to know how to do so many different things. It was a necessity. Sometimes she looks at me quizzically, and other times she gets it. It's those times of her getting it that make me feel I am carrying on the tradition of passing on those old-school skills. It is more than the skill that we pass along to those we are willing to have patience with. It is the spirit behind that skill that is the real-life lesson. Fearlessness, independence, and confidence—that's the lesson.

The Summer of Strawberry Rhubarb Pie

Part 2

"Mom, Mom, Mommy?" I heard my youngest, Clara Mae, call out to me as she blasted through the screen door, leaving it banging behind her. I shook my head and wondered, *What was she into now?*

It was the darndest thing about our Clara Mae. The summer Celia Simms passed away, I discovered that I was pregnant. Having lost a baby a year after Jon was born, I'd pushed the thought of another pregnancy to the very far reaches of my list of wants. One year turned to two, and so on. Then Maddie happened into our lives when Jon was six and she was four. With Jon almost twenty and Maddie seventeen and about to graduate from high school, there we were, about to start over. For all the milestones there were in life, being forty-three and pregnant had not been on that list.

The past seven years had flown. Clara Mae was a spitfire of a little thing, challenging everything that got in her way from day one. With her, our family dynamics changed on a daily basis. Maddie had first elected to go to community college while working for a local veterinarian's office and was currently in her residency year at Tufts and on her way to being a veterinarian. And Jon had enlisted in the Marines, had become a pilot, and was now attached to Homeland Security. He was always in a location that couldn't be divulged, but he was home on most holidays and often for no reason at all.

Things in town had changed, as they always do. We'd lost both Milly and Blanche in the same year. Milly went first at nearly 103.

When I visited Blanche after Milly's funeral, she'd told me she was waiting for a message from Milly to let her know what the next life was all about. I continued to visit her each week after church where we talked about people and how we were destined for something special: me due to my writing, and she because she was just damned old. "And besides," she'd say, "I want to see them try and put one hundred candles on my cake." She'd gotten her wish that day in August: one hundred cupcakes, each with a candle. She was tickled beyond belief. The last time I'd spoken with her, she'd told me she was ready. She'd had a dream about Millie who told her that they had a woman preacher up there that she liked and that she missed her. And yes, I did sing her little ditty as we said goodbye to her and tucked her in next to her husband and her daughter who had been my friend.

"I'm in the kitchen," I answered and listened as Clara Mae's backpack hit the floor and she ran down the hall. I was turning out a couple of pumpkin breads from their pans onto cooling racks. I'd made a strawberry rhubarb pie earlier, and that was cooling on my cake stand.

"Smells spicy," she said as she came around the corner and gave me a waist hug. She looked at the breads and wrinkled her nose. "Will I like it?" At seven, her taste buds were still developing.

"I think so. You like my banana bread. So it's almost the same, except instead of bananas I used pumpkin. And I'm making some honey butter to go with it." Trying to explain the different types of baked goods to her was more a test of my salesmanship skills than baking talents.

"Are there chocolate chips in it?" she asked and narrowed her dark-brown eyes as she studied the breads.

"No, honey. But there's raisins and pecans," I answered and hoped this would entice her.

"I don't like pecans." She tightly folded her arms around her middle and gave me that *try again, Mom* look.

"Really? You ate them last week in your oatmeal. Or did you forget?" I reminded her. I put the pans in the sink and ran the water to let them soak.

"Those were just nuts. I like just nuts. I don't like pecans." Her arms were still folded, her chin tilted up in the air as if to say, *take that.*

"That's okay. There'll be more for Daddy and me," I answered and waited for that to sink in.

"But what will I have for a treat?" She was now quite concerned.

"Well, I can make you some toast with jam. How would that be?" I continued washing the pans, but I could see her little brow furrow into a frown. She twirled the curly end of her left braid, a sign of her intense thinking.

"That's it?" She was quite dismayed.

"Yes, I'm afraid so." I could see her weighing her options.

"I bet other kids have more choices than toast." She had now taken a seat at the kitchen table and was drawing in the margin of the newspaper.

"You're probably right. But today you have a choice between toast with jam or pumpkin bread," I replied.

"I bet the Tooth Fairy or Mrs. Claus would have better things than that," she said as she looked up at me and sucked in her cheeks, a motion that she did when she was thinking. Ah, the mind of a seven-year-old. What do I say to this?

"That may be so, but things might be a lot different if you lived with them," I answered and wondered how long our verbal tug of war was going to last.

"Oh no, I think it would be lots of fun." She smiled up at me as if she had just read the highlights in the brochure for *Life with The Tooth Fairy*.

"I'm not so sure. There'd be lots of work to do. You'd have to help with the teeth," I said, trying to be a step or two ahead of my dear Clara Mae.

"Help with the teeth? Ewww!" Her little face crinkled up in horror.

"Sure, you'd need to sort and clean them. And then don't forget about the money." My creative writing instructor would have appreciated my quick thinking.

"Sorting teeth? Money? I'm only seven. I can't work. I would only be there for the treats." She had a very serious look now.

"I'm not sure what kind of treats The Tooth Fairy would have. There would probably be fruits and vegetables, so that your teeth would be healthy and not fall out." I started to make some honey butter for the pumpkin bread. Clara Mae watched me as I softened the butter and then beat in honey and cinnamon.

"Hmmm," she said and then asked. "But what about the money? What do you mean?"

"The Tooth Fairy leaves money, right?" She nodded and was now fascinated by what I was saying. "She'd need help keeping track of how many children she'd have to visit each night and how much money she'd have to leave each one. It's a big job."

"But I don't know anything about money. Maybe being with Mrs. Claus would be better." She'd gotten up from the table and come over to the counter where I was working. She laid her arm on the counter and inched her hand toward the butter to sneak a finger lick. I dipped a teaspoon in and gave it to her. She quickly put in in her mouth and smiled at me.

"Mrs. Claus has a lot of work to do. Think of all the elves she has that help her. If you were at the North Pole, you'd need to have a job there too. What do you think you'd be able to make?" I asked her.

"But it's not Christmastime now. I don't know how to make anything, I'm only seven. And aren't they on a baycation?" she protested. I smiled at her use of the word "baycation." Ever since she could talk, the word vacation had come out baycation, and now it had become an accepted family word.

"They work all year long to make sure the toy shelves will be full for Christmas," I said. She was thinking. I waited.

"But there'd be good treats. There'd be candy and cookies and all that stuff that Santa puts in my stocking." She was quite perplexed.

"Mrs. Claus makes those treats just before Christmas Eve, so they're nice and fresh. If she made them now, they wouldn't taste very good, would they?" I explained, and now she let out a heavy sigh.

"It sounds yucky," Clara Mae finally deduced. She had continued to stand at the counter, and now her little shoulders gave up in dismay.

"Things aren't always as they seem, honey," I said and bent down to give her a hug. I felt her snuggle into my neck as I held her. She released herself and went back to the table and her newspaper doodling. I plated one of the breads and sliced off the crusty end. I spread a bit of the honey butter on it and sighed as I enjoyed that warm bite of fresh baked goodness. Clara Mae was watching me as I chewed.

"Mommy, can I have a taste of that pumpkin bread?" she asked as she looked up.

"Why, of course," I answered and smiled. I sliced a piece, spread it with butter, and handed to her. She took it in her two little hands, closely examined it, and then tentatively nibbled the smallest of bites. I had to turn back toward the counter to hide my silent laughter. What a range of reactions she displayed. Suspicion, eyes widening, and finally acceptance, although I was not sure if it was total acceptance. I let her eat for a bit while I brought myself under control.

"So?" I asked and waited. I saw that she had eaten the entire piece and was using her finger to dab at the crumbs on the tabletop.

"I liked it, but I still like just nuts," she replied. It was as if she'd just begrudgingly delivered a one-star Michelin review to my kitchen.

"Okay, I'll remember next time to use just nuts." I turned my attention to the pie to see how cool it had gotten.

"Did you make that pie for Daddy?" Her brown eyes were smiling at me.

"No, honey, it's for a funeral. Liz's mom, Momma B, passed away," I answered and started to plan out answers to the probable questions of a seven-year-old. Liz's mom had always found time to visit with us on holidays. Christmastime was her favorite time to visit. She would spend several days making cookie baskets for all the kids in the neighborhood.

"What does *passed away* mean?" In all her seven years, there had only been two deaths in our family. One had been my dad, when Clara was only a month old. And the other had been our dog, Sandy.

We'd had Sandy since Maddie was twelve. She'd been one of several puppies in a box at the supermarket, and Maddie had instantly fallen in love with Sandy. Advertised as a golden retriever and something special, she became our funny girl with lustrous golden fur and the bowed legs of a basset hound. Our faithful pooch had grown up with Maddie and then had turned her attention to Clara. Always the sentry, she was ever-present by her side. She'd crossed the Rainbow Bridge last year. Clara cried when we explained that while Sandy looked like she was sleeping, she wasn't going to wake up. Tears had run down my face as I watched her tenderly stroke the fur of her loving protector. She had laid her head on Sandy's still soft fur as she cooed a farewell. "I love you, Sandy." My heart ached for this wonderful dog whose only need had been to love and be with us.

"Remember when Sandy went to heaven last year?" I watched as her face grew serious.

"Is Momma B going to see Sandy?" Her innocence was finding some hope.

"I'm pretty sure she will." What could I say? I was on the verge of tears spilling down my face as this spunky little thing was trying to reason the consequences and opportunities of passing.

"I'm sure Sandy will be able to sniff her out. I remember she gave Sandy cookies all the time. And Maddie told me that animals never forget the ones who feed them." Her face was full of certainty.

"I'm sure she will too, honey." I was about to change the subject, when *the* question came.

"Will we all 'passed away,' Mommy?" Her eyes watched me as I searched for all the answers that there were in the universe. Which one to choose? I drew in a breath and went for the simple one first.

"Yes, we all will someday," I said, and her eyes grew wide.

"But when? Do we all go together? I don't want to be here if were not together." Her lower lip started to quiver. I sat down in the chair next to her and pulled her up onto my lap. I looked into those loving eyes and stroked her hair away from her face.

"Oh now, it's going to be a long time, Clara, before any of us have to think of that." I rocked her and held her little body softly next to me. I rested my head on top of hers and kissed it.

"But what if—" I put my finger to her lips.

"No more today. Come on, let's go outside and look for a new spot to make your summer fairy garden." I gently slid her off my lap and put her hand in mine, and we walked out into the sunshine of a bright afternoon.

My Summer Bathtub Boat

The water is so warm.
The tub is just my size.
Enamel on metal, white, with
A crack in one spot
My chubby fingers pick at the crack
To get to the blue underneath.

Leaves from the butternut tree above
Offer shade and sun, and summer breeze lifts their frond-like leaves
I play in the water.

My father toils in the garden. My mother hangs
clothes from the fraying rope lines.
She uses a forked board to hoist
My father's heavy work clothes
The wind billows the sheets like
Sails on a land locked boat

I am happy in my little boat
Sailing along the green grass ocean

Mornings at The Lake

The breakfast symphony has started.
Silverware causes a shrill clatter
Making you hungrier that you thought you were.
Hard cereal creates a small avalanche of high-pitched tones
Tumbling into the bowl
The meal is on the deck today.
The solo diner clutches a sweater to herself
Until the morning sun warms her being.

A screen door slams at one location
The click of the canine's paws on the deck and down the stairs,
Carries his percussion section of his tags
And other trappings of the modern-day pooch
Who has everything to chew on, to sit on, to wear,
Because his owners think this is what he needs.
Now the dog rustles through the undergrowth
Woods where he will lie on the damp and dewy leaves…content.

A rhythmic "soleful" sound comes from the roadway
Announces the beginning of the daily exercise.
From now until dusk they will come
In all forms of footwear, walking, running, blading, biking
And every now and then the occasional individual strolls
For not the want of perceived self-motivated need of proving,
For he can be, just he.

The water ripples and slaps against my fortress.
The source still indistinguishable as yet,
But someone or something has broken the mirror like surface
It has announced to all that they are HERE!
Moments later I hear the paddle,
A regulated dipping, and then the repeated surging of the canoe
It slides past me to greet the sun.

The wind has tempted the sailboat to swing and bounce
It demands that time be made for its next voyage.
The clips clang against the mast with its impatience,
As if to say "I want to go, now."

The wind blows over my body, delivering a quick chill.
My hero, the sun, moves in to show its
strength and warms the chill away.
The slats from the chair have found a
comfortable position along my back
As they are ready themselves for their supporting
role in my quest for relaxation.

Morning, this morning on Alexander Lake is the best so far
Tomorrow morning, may be better
Everything is better at The Lake

The Book of I Am

The Book of I am, an assignment
That a friend asked her dinner guests to do.
Structure any way we wanted;
Prose, poem, or short story, about you.
It is an interesting exercise

Introduction
I am from strong women and men.
Stubborn and as subtle as a hangover.
Quiet and soft as a snowflake in winter in Bozeman
Hearty food, faded homemade clothes, warm soil
I am sure they would never understand my book

Chapter One
Wrong thing
For the wrong reason
At the wrong time
I am stable, steady, as all around me were in a haze
Not the time for a next generation
I am done with all of this

Chapter Two
Time is flying
A third of the way through
Try again, keep the smile, hide the tears
Stay strong,
I never give in
I never give up
Never again, I am gone

Chapter Three
Finally, the right beginning
So, near the end
Life and vitality and promise and strength
Discovering and unlocking the doors to the next book
So many pages to write
About hearty food, faded homemade clothes, and warm soil
So many ways to be I am

Epilogue
Turn the page, look ahead, look behind, and see where I am from

So You Want a Pet?

It is said that pets may be the only family member that you actually like. For those who have welcomed a creature of some type into their lives, the pleasure of the pet's company is infinite. For the rest of you, I hope that you may enjoy the following tale.

When we are growing up, we live in a home governed by adults. Whatever relationship they were to you, blood or otherwise, they were in charge. What you wear, eat, who you talk to, and play with. What you do on Tuesdays, and the list goes on and on; it is all prescribed by the adults. This was particularly applicable when it came to pets. Depending on when you entered your family, there may have already been a pet in residence. Which is great, so long as the pet accepted you and didn't think you were taking its place. The pet already belonged to someone, whether it be Dad's dog or Mom's kitty; whatever its affiliation, it was not yours. My father had hunting dogs. They were my buddies to some extent, but their loyalty and attention was ultimately toward my father.

You might have been lucky to have gotten your way when you begged and pleaded for that specific dog or cat with the promises to *always* feed and take it for a walk. I had a small metal bank on which I had scratched into its paint, *My horse fund*. I learned the law of diminishing returns, never quite being sure why my fifty cents a week never amounted to the many dollars needed to purchase the precious pony.

My parents were right. I never would have taken care of a horse. Even though we had other animals, a horse was not going to be part of this prepubescent girl's dream. As luck would have it, I had a friend who had horses. And her parents were happy to have me visit and try to ride their lovely mild-mannered ponies. Emphasis on the try.

Some horses are quite crafty when they sense a new rider. My horse, Checkerboard, was no exception when he distended his belly while I was cinching the saddle. I swear he laughed at me when he exhaled later on when we were crossing a stream. And of course, that exhale was all that was needed to send me around his chubby belly, landing me on my butt in the water.

As we mature, we move out of our childhood home and find one of your own. Whomever we room with, there are concessions for all types of things. Rugs, food, TV shows, love interests, and pets. One of my best friends had Rodney, a St. Bernard, and I had Lucy, a Persian cat. Not necessarily a match made in heaven, but it worked until the dog chased the cat into the road, and needless to say, it didn't end well for the driver of the vehicle. The cat escaped with nary a scratch. The Volkswagen beetle, however, needed a new door, and Rodney had a slight headache.

Moving on to settling into life and finding the mate, the "right one," a new living arrangement develops. Gone are the decorations of posters and pretty wine bottles, and you welcome in adult things that you both love, or at least agree to love.

And if arrangements allow, a pet can enter your world. So now this story will get down to more specifics.

Acquiescing to my husband, our first dog entered. Rigsy was a mongrel pup with traces of some German Shepard and lots of others. He was a sweet boy who liked to play and take long walks. If he had liked wine, he might have been the better spousal choice.

While we toiled at our jobs, Rigsy's walks more often than not ended up in the nearby Catholic church. The priests were kind and would quietly lead him out after the service. I learned of his regular church attendance through a friend's mother who laughed at this little dog who showed up for communion and tried to beg for a piece of host. Honestly, we did feed him!

The second dog came along after we moved from an apartment and bought a house. Rigsy had long passed over the Rainbow Bridge, and it seemed it was time for another pet. In came a puppy that was introduced as "Go see Mommy" and later named Cos (Crazy on Sunday). I was never sure where the pup had come from. But who could refuse a blonde bundle of fur with big eyes? What breed you ask? A pit bull terrier. I understood and was aware of the bad press for this breed, but Cos was different. We decided to not dock her tail and clip her ears. It was more a financial decision than it was to live her life incognito. She was an intelligent and fun girl. She loved her trips to the local drive-in hamburger joint for her cup of vanilla ice cream. People would stop and remark about what a good dog she was. And when the inevitable question came—what kind is she—people would slowly back away. Which was fine with her; she was my protector, my girl, my foot warmer on my bed.

She did have a dalliance with the neighbor's Siberian Husky, however. The offspring were striking. Ice blue eyes, thick blonde coats, and elegant plumed tails. When people asked about origins, we emphasized more of the Husky than her pit bull terrier side. Thankfully we had kept her incognito status to protect the innocence of the puppies.

Easter of that year brought the need for some type of activity. I had explained to my mate that we needed something for the girls, and he was quick to say he could handle this. While I had visions of foil covered chocolates and sitting down to color eggs, he had other ideas. Enter baby bunnies. Adorable as they hopped around on the couch, they tried to find where their baby bunny food was going to be. It wasn't going to be in the couch cushions that they almost immediately started to munch on. They are extremely cute for Easter and about ten minutes on the next day. After that, reality, as always, sets in. What do we do now? They said they can be litter box trained. Sure, that's if they are big enough to hop into the litter box and understand the entire concept. Eventually, there was a rabbit hutch built where they enjoyed their short lives. Note to self: don't build the rabbit hutch near the pit bull's area. I'll spare you the details of the tragic ending, but let's say that children learn a lot about life through their pets.

Another of our more adversarial pet combinations were a Maine Coon cat, a pair of finches, and a beagle. An exotic three-tiered bamboo cage was the perfect home for the two tweeters. And tweet they did. Much to the enticement of the cat. Daisy, the beagle, couldn't be bothered with the birds, but ooh that cat! A couple of examples of *you're not going to believe this* are worth mentioning at this point.

The cage for the seed seeking tweeters was strung pully-like through a floor grate, so that it was suspended up high and away from kitty. Think old Cape-style home with grates to allow for the heat to rise from the first to the second floor. To cut down on the seed debris, an equally striking basket was fastened to the bottom of the cage. Picture a lovely winter morning, coffee cup in hand, purring kitty snug by the wood stove, and Daisy barking at everything that came into her yard. And then we heard it. Sudden, very odd screeks, which was followed by hysterical tweets from Mr. and Mrs. Finch. As we entered the room, here was the cat, who had managed to prove that cats can jump, with all four paws affixed to bottom of the basket, swaying wildly back and forth. I imagine that she realized her folly when she tried to reach up toward her prize destination and found, to prove another adage, that cats do land on their feet.

One of the birds—I'm sure it must have been Mr. Finch—was unable to stand the stress of the attack. He was given a proper burial, with animal military honors. The girls insisted that he had been in the Air Force. We played taps on the kazoo. They cried; we bought another bird.

Throughout the spring and summer months, the new Mr. Finch was thrilled with his new mate and housing arrangements. We weren't quite sure about Mrs. Finch's feelings, but they seemed happy and hadn't asked for any counseling, so all was well. They were enjoying their summer on the porch, which was protected from the ever-conniving kitty. In August, I had an occasion to travel for work and was to be out of town for a few days. There was a checklist for food in the fridge and reminders for the feeding and watering of our menagerie. The list was met with "don't you worry, they'll be fine, I can handle this."

When I returned home, I was greeted with welcoming woofs from my stinky beagle, furry kitty twining herself around my legs, and a big hug from my husband and the girls. As I put my things down, I asked, "And how are Mr. and Mrs. Finch?" Stone silence as his eyes widened, and a look of terror filled his face. I didn't wait for him to speak. I ran to the porch door, opened it, and listened. All was silent, and so, too, were Mr. and Mrs. Finch. Kazoos in hand, another burial with military honors was conducted, and a decision was made that birds would be off the approved household pet list.

The stories could go on and on from ferrets to fish to toy fox terriers. I have cleaned, fed, groomed, and taken care of many types. And that's just the husbands. But as I settle into the later years of my life and reflect on the numerous pets that I have held for those precious moments in time, I have this to share.

All creatures great and small enter our homes not knowing anything about a human's life. They don't understand our voices. They know that no one knows their language. Unless you have a multiple pet household with one of their kind, it must be like being the only one of your kind in the world. We humans have a duty to care for them and teach them. Our animal's behavior is a reflection on us. If we allow them into our laps or on our counters when we're alone with them, then they see no difference in performing that same way when we have company.

Remember, they don't know how to operate a can opener, clean their litter area, or turn on the faucet. Oh wait, I did have a cat who was quite accomplished with a faucet. But by and large, our pets are the part of our family who will always need us for these basic necessities of life.

During the COVID pandemic when were hunkered down, the number of cats and dogs that were adopted, fostered, and rescued increased by more than twenty-five percent. Correspondingly, an increase in veterinarian visits was noted, helping these new pet owners understand how to care for their pet. New pet parents came to acknowledge that there was more to having a pet than cuddling with their furry friend and finding the newest pet toys online. Pets, like humans, needed medical care to keep them healthy and to be a member of the family, even if the family was just you and your pet. I also note unfortunately that some pets have been given up for adoption due to a lack of so many things that we humans have faced in the past two years. The majority, however, are still with their families, being a part of everyday life.

I believe an animal—and I am partial to cats—provides us with companionship, diversion through their antics, and the ability for us to care about something other than ourselves. We all need a reason to be something to someone every day. And if that someone is a pet, we must choose carefully when that time comes to invite a furry or feathered creature into our lives. Good training, grooming, and health care are essential to both you and your two or four-legged friend. Be the reason that an animal thrives and lives to a ripe old age.

Now excuse me, it's time to feed my cat.

The Monuments of Names: An Observance of Veterans Day

It was a cold November morning several years ago. The weather was drab and dreary. Somewhere between a heavy gray mist and a light rain fell as I made my way to the group of people who were gathering. I wished I'd worn a warmer coat.

It was Veterans Day, and I wanted to see the new monument that had been erected in the larger town near where I'd grown up. Friends of mine who'd served during Viet Nam were from that town. I hoped I might see someone from fifty years ago. Our town had yet to raise enough money to place their own memorial to those who had served after WWII. The VFW had continued to hold its various fundraisers, but there was never enough money to complete the task.

This new monument was situated in line with the other war memorials on the green near the high school. It was to honor those who had served after the Korean Conflict. It was about ten feet high and three feet wide and was draped in a black cloth. A group of men and women were walking around it to see if they could catch a glimpse before the unveiling. They were veterans of various ages and likewise, in as many stages of health. Wheelchairs, crutches, and walkers almost outnumbered those who could walk on their own. The conversations were genuine as they shook hands and embraced their old friends. I heard bits and pieces of tête-à-têtes as they reminisced. Conversations that held many smiles while others concluded with heads lowered and shaking as they heard sad news of another's departure.

The older service women wore comfy shoes and warm coats. A couple of younger veterans, fit and trim, were clad in their dress uniforms and looked like they had just finished a parade march at their academy. There was an unmistakable scent of mothballs from the older men. Their navy suit jackets had been pulled out of the closet for today's special occasion. Some struggled to fasten the worn gold buttons around their rotund bellies, a life that bespoke of good meals. Others showed definite signs of ill health as their clothes hung on thin frames, almost fluttering like curtains in a summer breeze. Lapels held commemorative pins and remnants of potluck suppers. Younger veterans wore bomber jackets embroidered with their conflict service years and had baseball caps on their heads. Whether it was a cloth cap or baseball cap, all were embroidered in gold with their post numbers, service branches, and dates of their service.

The arrival of the dignitaries signaled the imminent start of the ceremony. Standing near the monument, they shook hands with those closest to them. Some of them also wore their caps indicating their service. A woman hurried toward the front with a small portable PA system and quickly set it up. As the speaker crackled to life, I was struck by the way the veterans automatically assembled into formation. Those in wheelchairs, walkers, and crutches were helped to the front by the others who were more mobile. Metal folding chairs were opened and placed for those who couldn't stand. The remainder fell in behind them, their backs a little straighter, their shoulders squared.

The weather began to worsen. The light precipitation now progressed to a steady cold rain. I, along with a few others, opened our umbrellas and stood behind the veterans. The speakers welcomed and thanked those in attendance. They thanked the towns and organizations for the contributions to erect this monument. The local post commander next addressed and thanked the veterans, both present and those who had paid the ultimate price for freedom. He spoke of the extreme sacrifices in their service to our country throughout our history. And to those who were currently serving, he offered prayers for the safe return to their homes when their duty was over.

In silence, with a slight tug, the monument's silken drape was allowed to flow to the ground. The insignias for each branch of the service had been carved into the top of the elegant stone. The names were displayed in two columns. Beside each name was the year of the soldier's death.

As the commander began the roll call, I watched as those men and women in front of me raised their right hands in a stiff and unwavering salute. The rain rolled off their caps and onto their shoulders. The water sank into the fabric, at first becoming small blotches. As more and more drops fell, those proud shoulders became saturated. But still they held themselves in attention for their fallen brothers and sisters. The water dripped off the fronts of their caps and ran down their noses, and still they remained in their salutes of honor.

The next name hit me. Molly Angela Blake. What? No! I heard the name of my high school friend and inhaled deeply. We'd lost track of each other after she'd joined the Navy and I'd gone off to college. I'd wondered why she'd never come to our class reunions. I always thought she'd made a career of the service and was too far away. I hadn't realized she'd died in combat.

We were members of our high school track-and-field team. We were the "big girls," throwing shot put and javelin and running the long relays. We'd often joked about how we were going to outrun the "gazelles" of our team, as we were built for the long haul. She would always look over her shoulder and urge me to try to catch her, laughing and calling me names. Those sturdy freckled legs pumping and her red ponytail swinging side to side as she ran.

I'd lived next to the school, so most days after practice she'd stop over for whatever food my mom had left for us that day. We'd devour it, do some homework, and then head out. Molly lived about two miles away, so I'd run halfway with her to keep her company and then run back home. All the while she was yelling how she'd beat my butt the next day.

I smiled briefly as I thought of her running through the clouds past all the gazelles. I looked around to see if her brother was here. No one—only me to hear her name. I clutched my collar closer around my neck to chase a shiver.

With a haunting rendition of Taps, the ceremony concluded. The veterans stepped forward to get a closer look. Some pressed their hands to certain names on the monument, while others moved away in silence. Farewell embraces were held a bit longer, as eyes brimming with tears looked into the knowing eyes of the other. I took hold of and shook the calloused hand of one man as he was about to walk away and said, "Thank you for your service." As he looked at me, he wiped his eyes and patted the top of my hand. I smiled at him through the tears in my eyes. No other words were spoken. I stepped forward to touch Molly's name and said a silent prayer as my fingers touched the cold stone.

I realized that each man and woman there on that day was their own monument. Like that big black stone, they had the names of those they'd fought alongside with etched into their souls. They remembered the faces that bore the pain of the war. But they could also recall the times when they had shared a smile, a picture, or a story from home. Those were the way they had kept the ugliness of war at bay.

I remembered my father laughing and telling me tales about the men he'd served with, but never the stories of horrors he had lived through. There were times when he'd have that serious faraway look that belied his otherwise happy countenance. He kept several old black-and-white photos of handsome young men standing at attention. Others captured the weariness of the day: arms around shoulders, cigarettes dangling from mouths, halfhearted smiles. He'd call them by their nicknames; Shorty, Buster, Gunslinger, and others that I couldn't remember now. The lucky ones had come home to their girlfriends and started their families—the families that were here today, listening for their name. The others, they were the ones my dad had called the heroes. They were the ones whose names were said today with no one to hear of their courage.

I observed that Veterans Day that I had no understanding at all of what it takes to serve in our military. I was embarrassed at my discomfort for the past half hour or so due to the weather. What these soldiers had endured for their years in combat and service—waiting and watching in the rain, snow, and heat, the unimaginable horrors of war—was all in the name of defending freedom, our freedom. These men and women who had assembled in front of me were our American heroes. They were the ones who, through their dedication, made this the land of the free and our home, their home, the home of the brave.

A Trio of Beachgoers

We're a trio of beachgoers
Each of us enjoying this moment.
Little is said.
We look at one another.
We smile.

My grandmother's black skirt flutters in the ocean breeze.
The stockings she wears are heavy, to
compress her painful bulging veins
Her stockinged toes stick out of her sturdy black lace-up sandals
She sits in a striped canvas chair, shaded by a striped
canvas umbrella, clamped to the wooden arm.
She squints toward the horizon, over the Sound past the
waves, searching, like the wife of a seafaring man.
Remembering her first trip across that ocean
that brought her to America.
She smiles.

My mother wears a stretched out blue bathing
suit, a byproduct of her Rubenesque body.
She sits on the wool blanket, topped with
her threadbare striped beach towel.
"Still good enough for the beach," she says.
She is busy comforting her mother and watching for me.
She has left the household worries behind.
She watches the water; she's looking for
me. I wave, she knows I'm fine.
She smiles.

I swim, buoyed by the saltwater. The water is a second home to me.
I frown because we have come to this beach, the
one that has no waves, no surf, just gentle waves
that my mother feels safe enough to swim in.
I watch her as she opens the cooler that contains
our lunch and I leave the water.
I smile.

The green and silver metal cooler is opened.
It contains wax papered sandwich bags.
The sandwiches are almost soggy now from the ice packs.
Spam salad on white bread.
Store-brand potato chips, slightly stale,
because they were saved for this day.

The thermos is round and green and plaid and drips
punch as I hold my flimsy cup under the spigot.
Saltwater dripping down my face onto my sandwich and
into my cup of red punch that will soon stain my lips.
We each have our sandwich and our punch.

Each of us enjoy this moment.
Little is said.
Life away from today at the beach is different.
It is hardship.
It is sorrow.
It is not always sunshine and red punch.
The burdens of life disappear as grains of
sand wash away from the shore.
We look at one another.
We smile.

The Woman with Two Purses

You look

Alone,
Worried,
Normal.

Your look
Is
Searching.
For a person,
For a sound,
For a motion.

Others stare back
Some blankly,
Some quizzical,
Some smiling.

You have

Your things, your coat, your purse, your book
Your emotions.

But…

I have

Extras,
Another purse, another coat
Another person's well-being.

We are there,
It's a doctor's office
Or a waiting room in a hospital,
Outside the treatment room.

I sip
Stale coffee,
Luke warm water,
Diluted soda.
I taste
The flavor of anticipation of bad news.

And then
I am beckoned.

I hurriedly gather
Our things.

I am a woman
With two purses
With two sets of feelings.

They watch you
Walk away and into that room
But with little interest.

Inside.

The truth and the lies begin.
The truth is the why.

But…

The lie begins with
How?
How long will it take?
How long will it be before she is able?
Able to
Be?

The rhetoric begins.

I hear, but hear no more.

The pain, is not my pain.
The pill is your pill.
The injection is your injection.
The hair loss is your hair loss.
The scarring
Yours is visible
Mine is hidden

But…
I wish there was a pill to relieve the pain and
the loss that has begun to scar you.

The Face.

Uplifted toward me
With hope,
With a slight smile,
With a hollow, long look coming from those
once comforting brown eyes.

The Body.

When did it start to look Frail?
To stoop,
To die.

When did it begin to rely on me?

The Mind.

How does it still know I am afraid?
How does it still know how to hide the deepest feeling?
How does it know when to give up?

The Journey.

I had hoped it would be longer.
For her, it is too long.
I wanted more bright spots.
She tries to remember the bright spots from before.

Before she was able to be independent,
Before she heard the truth and when the lies began.

The End.

Is never when it should be (As if you have control)
Is always a reality,
Is always the end and never a beginning?

And I will never carry a purse again…

My Seventy-Year-Old Ears

What the heck! Are my ears getting bigger? Oh no! I'm turning into my mother! I look at her picture and size up the situation. They do—my ears are starting to look like hers. I swear just yesterday these perfect pieces of pink cartilage were the host to some of the most unique ear art ever to be imagined. From strawflowers during the sixties, large colorful disks and dangles that made matchy-matchy of my outfits throughout the seventies and into the eighties, and finally settling on precious gemstones surrounded by gold or silver.

I really blame my mother. Of course, she had protected them throughout my childhood with the warmest of hats and earmuffs. Made sure they were cleaned inside and out. Took me to our family doctor to have them flushed out with some type of apparatus that resembled a caulking gun. And even on rare occasions had pulled on them to impress upon me some type of punishment for a minor infraction of my childhood experiences.

To assure myself that I was not alone in this lobe lengthening struggle, I did some research. Which is good because my mom is now off the hook. I'm sure she is looking down from heaven. pleased to know that I solved the problem. The real culprit here is gravity. Yup, good old gravity. It is documented that our ears lengthen at a rate of up to 0.22 millimeters per year. Don't stress the math. With Siri's help, that converts to 0.86 inches! Yikes! And it's not just our ears; it happens to our noses too!

But here's the silver lining in our aging plight. There's more ear to hear! From the laughter of our friends and family, to the whispers of our dearest, saying "I love you." The newborn grandchild saying "Mama," and the strains of our favorite music, turned up just a bit because we can. And yes, there will be sad news from time to time that we will wish we'd never heard; this is life.

Listening is our way of understanding each other. The better listener we are, the more we understand and communicate with each other. To paraphrase Roy T. Bennet, "Listening to someone may be all they need that day to turn their day around." And what better way to do that than with big ears!

The Woman with Two Purses Part 2

I am here again
Waiting, holding her purse
So, she can use her cane
When did she become older, frail?
Forgetful
Today she said
I can't find…
What can't you find? I ask
Let me help you
I can't remember,

I know it was right here, she says
What was it? I ask
I can't remember.

When we wait, she looks
Worried, but unaware,
She gives me a smile
I reach out
And pat her hand

*I could have driven
You know,*
I know.

I hold her purse
It's so heavy
What's in here?
Just things I need

Sunglass pouch dangles from the side
Old baggies with mints and candy, bank deposit
slips, and Band-Aids and Kleenex and
Where are my keys?

I have them
Are you sure?
Show me and I oblige
Good

The Last Sail

If you could wish…
To sail forever just you and I
With no changes changing
Except the sky

Where our smiles are constant,
The norm for the day
And nothing can ever take that away

The sound of the water
The warmth of the sun
Our senses are full, so overcome

The simplest is best
We both would agree
If we could be wishing, for you and me

Never a dark cloud
Or the end of day
I only want things to be this wishing way

Remember our love
And the warmth of my hand
The touch that will linger as time begins to span

If I could wish
For you and I
Our words would be complete without the word…goodbye

The Summer of Strawberry Rhubarb Pie

Part 3

The living room looked like it was inhaling and exhaling as the summer breeze blew the curtains back and forth. How could it be June already? Clara had completed her sophomore year of high school and was working for Maddie this summer as a veterinarian tech. When she'd graduated from Tufts, Maddie had partnered with our town vet, Lois Fuller. Upon retiring Lois offered the practice to Maddie. And so, with the help of her parents' insurance policy, Maddie now had her own veterinary practice. The office and kennels had an apartment attached to it, but Maddie had chosen to stay home and rent it to Brewster. He was at Mountain State coming into his fourth year of veterinary studies. As payment for the room, Brewster was there to take care of the animals who were boarded overnight. It was a great arrangement for the both of them.

Jon was still with Homeland Security and was due home for the 4th of July with his girlfriend. And there was a promise that she was the one. Joe was now a partner in Lewis' Farm Equipment and Supply business and was away upstate at a two-day agricultural fair. I had published two more books with moderate success. It seemed I made just enough to pay for all the edits and licenses to begin the process all over again for the next one. I'd been a little tired lately, but I attributed that to the fact that I was sixty and had a thirty-five-year-old son, a thirty-three-year-old daughter, and a seventeen-year-old daughter who still had two more years of high school before she went on to her next adventure. So on this lovely day in June, it was just me, the girls, and Bruce.

Bruce was a big old orange tiger cat who'd been dropped off at Maddie's office more than five years ago. He'd gotten his tail caught in something and had been brought in by one of our church members. While it wasn't her cat, she'd been trying to nurse him back to health, but could tell he wasn't getting any better. Bruce stayed at the clinic for about a month, recovering from his tail infections which, to his dismay, had to be removed. With nobody asking about him, Maddie and Clara decided to bring him home to meet the rest of us. He had been happy to become that next member of our family. Currently, he was curled up on the couch at my feet.

"Maddie, a little help in here, puleeeese!" Clara wailed at the top of her lungs. I swear that girl never had a hushed tone in her life. Oh, I do take that back. When she'd gotten caught, oh so many times, her apology of "I'm sorry and I won't ever do it again" was the softest voice you could ever want to hear.

"What is it now, Clara?" Maddie was outside, hanging laundry on the clothesline, and Clara was in the kitchen. The shouting continued.

"Ya gotta come help me. I can't figure this out!" Her voice pleaded for her older sister's assistance. I could hear bowls and pans clanging and drawers being shoved in and out. I thought I also detected under her breath mumbles of some type of a seventeen-year-old's *I'm not supposed to swear, but I have to* comments.

"Mom's trying to sleep." Maddie's loudest whisper voice made me chuckle. Neither of them realized that the *mom's trying to sleep* ship had sailed the first moment Clara had loudly whispered to Maddie that she was going to bake a surprise for me. I decided to keep quiet and see how this episode of "Sisters in the Kitchen" panned out. I jotted a few thoughts down in my notebook. I was working on a compilation of cozy short stories, and these two were giving me more material than I'd ever thought possible.

I heard the screen door slam and then lowered voices. I kept my eyes closed to continue the ruse. I could tell by the weight of the walk that it was Clara who was trying to quietly tiptoe into the living room to see if I was asleep. The closer she got, the harder it was for me to keep from laughing. At the last moment I quickly reached up for her, she screamed, and Bruce shot off the couch like his butt was on fire.

"Mom, you scared me! And you're supposed to be sleeping!"

"Oh, my dear Clara. I'm so glad you aren't going into the secret intelligence service like your brother. They'd hear you coming half-way across the country." I sat up and pulled her down into a hug. "So what are you trying to make?"

"Aww, Mom. It's supposed to be a surprise." She screwed up her face and twirled her left braid, her tell that she was thinking.

"The way you two are carrying on, it would only have been a surprise if I'd gone on the trip with your dad." They both looked crestfallen that Clara's surprise had been blown.

"I can help her, Mom. Come on, Clara. Let Mom rest." Maddie pulled Clara up from the couch and put her big sister arm around her little sister's shoulders.

"It can still be a surprise. Let's do this—you can ask me any technical questions that you have, but I can't know what it is until it's finished." At this, Clara turned around, and her face brightened into a very broad smile. Maddie, who had learned all my baking tricks, gave me an all-knowing thumbs up.

"Come on, Clara, we got this." And thus Bruce returned to the couch, I opened my notebook, and the girls were back in the kitchen with the previous harsh kitchen noises quelled to good natured giggles. The baking sounds were now of chopping, mixing with that familiar bump and roll, the rhythmic cadence of my mom's old wooden rolling pin. This signaled that there was going to be some type of pie.

My girls made me smile. They were learning so much from each other. The seventeen-year age difference when Clara was born had caused a period of indifference for Maddie. While she loved her little sister, Maddie's sights on college in no way matched the neediness of Clara's as an elementary school child. For a time, with Maddie at college, we seemed to be two families. Maddie's calls were more adult: updates on the events of college life and classes. The frequency of returning home became occasional, as opposed to weekly when she'd first begun her studies.

In comparison to the parents of Clara's friends, Joe and I looked almost elderly. While Clara now reminded us that she kept us young, the comings and goings of playdates, birthday parties, and soccer practices were nonstop. Her love of animals coupled with the love for her sister had set her on a path to be following in her big sister's footsteps. This had now allowed Joe and me to have a bit of momentary calm.

As our sixties had started to roll in, there were days when I began to think about wanting to be at peace with my children's lives. With the service as Jon's second family, I knew my mother's worry about him was only when he was on an unknown assignment. He'd been gone now for half his life all over the world, so his homecomings were a time of different relationships. And now with the promise that he had found a mate, this only increased my feelings of peace for him.

With the girls, it was different. I remembered how lost Maddie had seemed when she'd come to us. Both parents gone and no family who wanted her. She'd called me Mama Sally for the first six months or so. But after hearing Jon only call me Mama, she soon dropped the Sally. Sometimes she would sit on my lap and hold both of my hands so tightly and then ask me never to let her go. It just broke my heart.

Maddie was ten at the time when we'd received a note from her cousin Kenny that his mom, her aunt Alice, had died of an apparent heart attack. The note had come after any service was held, so a visit to Vermont seemed pointless. We sat and talked about her real family after that note. The names of her cousins and her uncle were just that—names. No funny personality or stories to tell about the time when they did this or that.

There were times when she'd get angry and ask so many questions about why this had happened to her. As she got older, she tried to keep in touch with her Uncle Henry's kids in Montana, but that proved to be a lesson in futility. She'd sent cards for all the holidays for a number of years. But the only time she'd heard back from any of them was when her eldest cousin Bryan wrote to say that Henry had passed away. Her visits to her parents' grave had grown less and less as the years had gone by.

And now with her veterinary practice well underway, she had developed into an independent, caring young woman. One who was the best big sister, as Clara Mae had put it; and now as an adult, one of my best friends.

Clara had discovered the truth about Maddie's mom and dad when she was thirteen. It was after one of the times that Maddie had returned from the cemetery. I remember overhearing Clara asking Maddie where she'd been. Maddie asked her sister to come and sit with her out on the porch swing, so she could explain.

Clara seemed to be our family's glue. Every family has one; it just depended on the type of person a family needed. Your family's glue is different from the next family's. And sometimes there may be more than one. But when Clara was born, her presence seemed to have drawn us all closer than ever before.

My thoughts were again interrupted by Maddie's voice. But this time it was a cautious soft tone.

"Mama, there's someone at the door in a uniform and he wants to talk to you." Her beautiful face had so many questions. Maddie stood behind Clara, her hands on her shoulders as I quickly rose from the couch.

"Stay here, girls." And I approached the door with that feeling of dread that I'd hope would never have come.

*****

The morning of Jon's funeral, I rose just as the day was breaking through the night. It had been a week since the man in uniform had come to our door. The letter that I'd been handed that day informed us that Jon had been on assignment to rescue children who had been held captive for more than six months. He'd been one of three pilots flying helicopters for the mission. The other two had lifted off as he waited for that one last child. As soon as he took off, his chopper had been fired upon. It crashed and exploded on impact. All souls had perished. It also stated that Jon would receive the Navy Cross for his heroism and bravery.

I couldn't tell you what the man looked like, or what he said after he'd read the letter to me. After his first words of "I'm sorry to inform you that your son…" I froze into an eerie state of silence. It seemed like I'd stood there and held onto that letter for a year. I watched the dark SUV pull away slowly and eventually saw it disappear into the shimmer of the hot afternoon sun. How was I going to tell Joe? The girls? How could this have happened? Why our son? Jon had always been so selfless. Couldn't he have been spared?

We had all been numb the last several days as we went through the preparations for his funeral. We went from anger to hysterics. Long periods of silence had brief moments of normalcy. But we felt the guilt that all humans have when they realize normal isn't allowed anymore.

I put a pot of coffee on and thought about how many pies I needed to make today. Making pies had always been my time to reflect on the person who had passed. As I measured the flour into the bowl, the tears came like a flood. I held in my sobs as I stepped silently onto the porch. Bruce followed me, and as I sat down on the swing, he jumped up on my lap, allowing me to smother my tears with his purring. I couldn't do this, I just couldn't.

I heard footsteps coming from the side of the house and looked up as daylight was now bathing the porch with warm morning sun. With the sun behind the person, all I could see was an outline of a woman.

"Hello, Sally. I'm sorry to disturb you, but I saw your light on. I knocked at the front door, but no one answered. Jon had told me that I could always find you in the kitchen at the back of the house. I'm Caroline, Jon's wife," her quiet voice said.

"You're who? He said he'd finally met the right person, but he never—" I wiped my tears with my sleeve as I motioned for her to take a seat. She had long blonde hair and was dressed in loose sweats bearing the Marine logo. Even in the early morning light and through a tear-streaked face, I could see she was exceptionally pretty. She wore a wide band of gold on her left hand.

"I know. I told him he should have let you know, but he thought our big surprise would have really topped off the 4th of July celebration." Tears ran down her face as I got up and pulled her up into an embrace. It was then I noticed her protruding belly through those baggy sweats. My eyes went from her baby bump to her face as she tried to smile through her tears. She nodded, and I hugged her again even harder.

"But when?" That question could have had so many answers.

"Well, let's see. We met about two years ago when we were assigned to the same unit. And then we started dating. We were married after I got back from assignment this past January. But because of his next duty, there was no time to come back home and let everyone know. I'm due in September. It's a boy. Jon Joseph, if that's okay with you." She wiped her tears, and her lips quivered.

"Oh, my dear, Caroline. How can this be?" My emotions ran up and down the hill from sorrow to joy. The screen door opened. It was Joe. His hair sticking up all over his head and the dark circles under his eyes showing the signs of a week of extreme grief. He'd thrown on a pair of gym shorts and a faded John Deere T-shirt.

"Good morning. We have a visitor, I see. I'm Joe, and you are?" He held his hand out to Caroline, who stood to shake it.

"I'm Caroline and I'm—" She took his hand in both of hers.

"She's Jon's wife." Unable to contain myself, I finished her sentence, choking back the words.

"His wife?" A look of astonishment could not be hidden. I heard more footsteps in the kitchen.

"Hey, what's all the noise?" Maddie was up and rubbing her eyes. She was dressed in a long T-shirt with a black lab on the front.

"Maddie, this is—" I began and was extremely surprised at the next words.

"Caroline, oh, I'm so sorry." And the two young women embraced as if they were long-lost friends.

"Wait, you two know each other?" I was incredulous.

"Jon introduced me to Caroline via Skype about a year ago," she answered with that look of one who'd just gotten caught with their hand in the cookie jar.

"And you never told us?" This time Joe was taking the lead in this conversational inquiry.

"Jon made me promise. It was going to be this big beautiful surprise next month. We had all kinds of plans—" And Maddie's voice trailed off.

"Who are you?" Clara Mae asked as she now shuffled onto the porch in her blue fuzzy slippers and oversized fleece pants and top.

"I'm Caroline." Caroline extended her hand to Clara, who was still in a teenager's sleepy trance.

"I'm Clara Mae. Hey, you've got Marine sweats, just like my brother Jon has." Her eyes were now observing the scene more carefully.

"Clara, this is Jon's wife," Maddie started to explain. Clara's eyes were really open now.

"What? But I thought he was bringing you to meet us for the 4th?" Her mouth hung open.

"Why don't we have some breakfast and we can talk all about this? Girls, set the table, please." And I switched gears as I hoped to get my family ready for today and the life beyond.

*****

Jon Joseph was born on Labor Day, a coincidence that was not lost on Caroline after struggling for more than ten hours. He was twenty-three inches long, weighed in at nine pounds even, had a tuft of blonde hair, and was the most perfect child we'd ever seen. Caroline had rented a condo near us prior to her medical leave and had equipped it with everything a captain's pay could bring. We'd even had the chance to throw her a surprise shower with some of our neighbors and church family just a week before JJ was born.

It was so wonderful to have a baby in the family again. We shared duties with Caroline's parents, Ellie and Herb, in those first few weeks. They had been here for JJ's birth, but had to return to their home in Hawaii after a month due to Herb's medical needs. Ellie was so torn, hating to leave her only grandchild. But they promised to return as soon as Herb's health improved.

As her leave was about to end, Caroline had decisions to make. She'd put in for a transfer to a base closer to us. But now being a single parent, she was hesitant to return to active-duty assignments. With her rank of captain and her master's degree in business, she was offered a part-time teaching position for the ROTC program at Upper State University. We were thrilled with this appointment as Upper State was only a half hour away.

As I sat and rocked JJ one day, I was sad when I thought about my handsome son. How was I ever going to tell JJ about him? It would come in time, I knew. Pictures and phone videos would keep Jon's face alive for his little boy. Our stories would fill in the rest. So now our family had a new glue, and it had come just in time.

I hoped that someday Joe and I might teach him all those skills that his father had been so good at: baseball and fishing and his wonderful sense of humor. Given the chance, I hoped I could show him how to bake, maybe even a pie. And then we could tell stories and look at pictures as we prepped the ingredients of his life pie.

How we prepare and witness those ingredients of life every day is up to us. We must mix just the right flavors and seal them in, so their goodness won't leak out. But we do need an outlet, so everything isn't bottled up inside too. And then waiting. Sometimes, that's the hardest part of all. However long our wait is, we need to continue making pies.

How else can we enjoy life one slice at a time?

I'm Not Ready

I want you to be
Better,
And I'm sure when I help you, when I tell you
When I explain why you must,
It will be no time
Before,
Before what?

Before you are still tired
Before you don't get better
Before I realize,
I want you to be better for me,

Because I'm not ready

Not ready to see you old
Not ready to see you not do the things you're supposed to do
The things you always did
The things I could never do

I'm not ready to lose you

I'm not ready
To miss you
To not be able to talk, or laugh or complain with you
To not have you to hug

To not have you…I'm not ready.

Heaven

First let me state that this writing has nothing to do with religion. Thus, I invite you to read on.

Several of the stories and poems that you have read in this book have dealt with the seasons of our aging process and sometimes, the ultimate end. So these final words seemed to me to be the appropriate conclusion.

It's hard to recall when you first heard the word heaven. Maybe you remember it from a prayer, "on earth as it is in heaven," or you overheard an anecdotal response of "for heaven's sake." Or it could be the explanation of where your cherished pet was now residing. And the ultimate of *someone up there is watching you.* Whenever the word or the notion of heaven made it into your world, you might have begun to wonder about heaven.

As you grew older and began to understand the event of someone's passing, your curiosity brought about many of the dreaded questions that adults hate to answer. From the *where are they?* to *can I go visit?* to *why*, we have asked these questions and answered them, all without really knowing.

On a recent visit to our son's home in Florida, my four-year-old granddaughter asked me about Ozzie, her favorite of my cats. Our lovely Ozzie had passed away after their visit at Christmastime, and while Mom and Dad knew, our granddaughter did not. I was now faced with *the* decision. What was the right way to answer? Besides her wondering blue eyes, there were three more sets of eyes focused on me. And they, too, were waiting for that response.

A million answers went through my mind. Should I say he's good and can't wait for you to come back and visit? Would the answer of *he's not feeling well* let her down gradually? But then that surely would be followed by many *what's the matter with him* type of inquiries. Finally, without too much lag time, I ripped the Band-Aid off and out my answer came. "He's in heaven." This was now followed by that nanosecond of silence as all eyes widened.

"Is he with Pop-pop, Grammy, and Ribby?" These were the three souls who she knew were now in heaven. Pop-pop, her grandfather; Grammy, her grandmother; and Ribby had been Mom and Dad's pet prior to Mom conceiving her.

"Yes, he is." I held my breath as my mind tried to triage the next set of questions. One category could be *how did he die*, another of *when*, and still another of *are you sad*. But I got none of these.

"What about Harriet? Doesn't she miss him?" She now directed her attention to Harriet, Ozzie's sister. I was relieved, but again I was on the roller coaster of the next possible scenario.

"She does." What else could I say?

And then here it came. "When are we going to heaven?" Her little brow scrunched up in concern. Eight eyes, three sets of blue and one set of green, all stared back at my dark-brown pools of grandmotherly solutions.

"Not for a long, long time, my dear. Now, I'm going to count to three before I chase you into the pool." And off I went, chasing this beautiful squealing child into the pool to splash and let the water wash away the veil of uncertainty about the unknown heaven. I thought I heard a collective sigh of relief as we padded our bare feet toward the pool. All were thankful that the discussion was over.

Not long after that visit, I found myself at a family member's funeral. In that beautiful church, I mused the whole idea of heaven. I was alone in my thoughts as the priest mumbled on. Looking at the ornate depictions of biblical beings floating on clouds above my head, it made me think of two things in childlike fashion. The first was that heaven has got to be really big. I mean depending on whatever you believe in, that's got to be a rather large piece of real estate. And the other was not about seeing or locating my family or friends. But if I got there and if heaven was all that I had heard about during my life—and assuming I went there—would I see all of my pets? Silly, isn't it?

Whatever your religion is, or lack thereof (I'm not judging. I label myself an occasional congregationalist because I like singing hymns), we all look to the sky at some point in our lives and wonder. We wonder about the shape of the cloud. We hope the cloud will come and give us some relief from the sun's hot rays. We might even wonder if those clouds really are heaven.

But we'll never know, and I suppose that's just how life is. If we knew about tomorrow, or next week or next year, our decisions would be so very different. We humans make plans, break promises, and hopefully come to appreciate or accept the way our lives turn out. It's up to us to make the best of our moments in the seasons of life.

And if heaven is truly real, then I will be ever so happy to see my beautiful Ozzie again.

The End

Recipes

STRAWBERRY RHUBARB PIE

Ingredients

2 cups of fresh strawberries, washed, hulled and sliced
2 cups of fresh rhubarb, chopped in one-inch cubes/slices
1/4 cup of Minute tapioca
1 1/4 cup of white sugar
1 teaspoon of orange zest
1 teaspoon of orange extract
1 teaspoon of ground cinnamon
Pie crusts for top and bottom of a 9-inch pie plate
One large egg
Water
1–2 tablespoons sugar

Mix sugar and tapioca in a large bowl.
Add fruit and remainder of ingredients. Mix and let stand for 15 minutes.

Preheat oven to 400 degrees.

Line the bottom of 9-inch pie plate with one crust.
Spoon filling into pie shell.
Place top crust on top.
Seal crust and crimp/flute the edges.
Cut several slits in the top crust to allow steam to escape.
Brush the top with an egg wash (one egg mixed with a tablespoon or so of water).
Top with sugar

Bake at 400 degrees for 45–50 minutes, or until juices form bubbles that burst slowly.
Let cool.
Serve with vanilla ice cream or whipped cream.

Dill Pickles (Refrigerator Processed)

Ingredients

2–4 cucumbers, depending on their size (freshest possible; cut to your desired shape: spears, or chunks)
3/4 cup Kosher salt
3/4 cup white vinegar
Dill, fresh: several sprigs and/or seed heads layered into the bottom of the jar
Dill, dried: 1/2 to 1 teaspoon
5 cloves of peeled and chopped garlic
8 cups hot water

Wash jars/containers.
If using canning type jar with screw-on bands, make sure to use new lids.
If recycling jars (relish or mayo) with screw tops, make sure both the glass and lids are clean.
If using plastic containers with snap-on lids, make sure the top fits securely.
Mix all ingredients, except the cucumbers, until the salt dissolves.
Place cucumbers snugly in the container. If using fresh dill, place the dill in the container first.
Pour liquid over the cukes. Cover with lid. Set aside to cool before refrigerating.
Cucumbers will continue to pickle in the refrigerator as the days go on: slight pickle, half sours, and then finally full dill.
Pickles can be stored in the refrigerator up to six months, if they last that long!

SWEET (BREAD AND BUTTER) PICKLES (REFRIGERATOR PROCESSED)

Ingredients

Vegetables (Select just ripe and slice to your bite-sized liking thickness; keep the size consistent in all 3 veggies used. Other veggies can be used as well—cauliflower, beans—use your imagination.)
2–3 Cucumbers (The number depends the size of the cuke. Slice bite-sized, thick or thin.)
Onion, 1 white or yellow (Slice bite-sized, thick or thin.)
1–2 pepper (Sweet red is best—a hot one if you like. Slice bite-sized, thick or thin.)
3 cups sugar
1/4 cup Kosher salt or less, depending on your liking
1 teaspoon turmeric
1 teaspoon mustard seed

Wash jars/containers.
If using canning type jars with screw-on bands, make sure to use new lids.
If recycling jars (relish or mayo) with screw tops, make sure they are clean—both the glass and lids.
If using plastic containers with snap-on lids, make sure the top fits securely.
Heat sugar, salt, and spices over medium heat until sugar and salt are dissolved.
Pack cukes and veggies snugly into container.
Pour liquid over the pickles. Cover with lid. Set aside to cool before refrigerating.
Pickles can be stored in the refrigerator up to six months, if they last that long!

PUMPKIN BREAD

Prepare 3 loaf pans—I use 3×5—by lightly greasing and flouring. Preheat oven to 350 degrees.

Ingredients

First

1 15-ounce can pumpkin
4 large eggs
1 cup vegetable oil
2/3 cup water
3 cups white sugar

Second

3 1/2 cups flour
2 teaspoons baking soda
1 1/2 teaspoons salt
1 tablespoon each of cinnamon and nutmeg
1/2 teaspoon ground cloves
1/4 teaspoon ginger

Third

1 cup raisins
1 cup chopped pecans

In a large bowl, mix all ingredients in the *first* section until well blended.
Add the ingredients in the *second* section a little at a time until just blended.
Remove bowl from mixing stand and add the *third*, raisins and pecans, mixing by hand. Mixture will be soupy!
Divide into the 3 prepared pans.

Bake for 50 minutes and between and 5 to 10 minutes longer, depending on the size of pan that you use. Toothpick should come out clean!
Let cool for 10 minutes before removing from pan, then cool further on wire rack.
Enjoy with a generous slather of Honey Butter.

Honey Butter

In a bowl, place:
1 softened stick of butter
1/8 to 1/4 cup of honey, depends on your sweet tooth!
1/8 teaspoon of cinnamon or vanilla

Combine using a hand mixer for a fluffy butter. Mix by hand for a sturdier butter.
Store in a covered container on the counter or in the refrigerator.
This can easily be doubled or tripled, placed in pretty containers, and used as a hostess gift.

Banana Bread with "Just Nuts"
(Clara Mae's Walnuts)

Prepare a 9×5 loaf pan by lightly greasing and flouring. Preheat oven to 350 degrees.

Ingredients

1 stick of butter
3 large eggs
3 or 4 ripe bananas, mashed
2 cups flour
1 teaspoon baking soda dissolved in a little cold water
1/2 to 1 cup of chopped walnuts
1/2 to 1 cup of semisweet chocolate bits

Combine ingredients in the order they appear in the list above, mixing well after each one.
Pour into prepared pan.
Bake at 350 degrees for 40 minutes. May take 45 to 50 minutes. Toothpick should come out clean!

By Jane Herr Desrosiers

Introduction

Coming Summer of 2024, The Gardener, The Old Man and The Cat. Jane Herr Desrosiers introduces us to a new cast of interesting characters in her latest cozy mystery. Meet Billie, the soon to be gardener for a lonely curmudgeon on Long Island. Her occupation turns from gardener to sleuth as she digs in and gets to the root of the mystery in Rose's research.

The Old Man, the Gardener, and the Cat

The Blackstone and Miller Growing Complex, near Ithaca, New York
March 1964

The sun was strong as it streamed through the shop's windows. It had stretched across the floor throughout the afternoon and had finally landed on the counter area. The light had caused the dull plastic greeting card rack to glisten like a prismatic crystal. It was four thirty now—time for the day to end. The retail shop had been bustling all day. And while Blackstone & Miller was a renowned rose-grower, pots of daffodils, tulips, and hyacinths had been the customer favorites of the day. Palm Sunday was this week, and even though the shop closed at four o'clock, the last patron was just leaving. Mrs. Blackstone went to the door, turned the lock, and flipped the door sign from Open to Closed.

The air was damp and fragrant with the scent from the bouquet of Easter lilies and red roses that the last customer requested. Rose had wrapped the bouquet and clipped the thorns from the stems of the roses. She was also mindful to remove the puffs of yellow pollen from the velvety white blossoms of the lilies. While customers thought the pollen was pretty, they realized often too late that it also stained fabrics. Rose was wiping the golden yellow pollen off her apron. She studied her stained fingers, wrinkled her nose, and thought how roses *wouldn't do this*. Her internal conversation continued, *And I won't have work here much longer. After all, I got accepted into the Cornell's School of Botany Masters Class. And with a little luck,*

I'm sure I'll be able to get that research job that was posted. She smiled to herself as she picked up the trash pail and brought it to the back room.

The workers from the shop and the greenhouses were gathered in the back of the store. This was where bouquets and arrangements were designed. Barbara, one of the high school student workers, was sweeping the floor of the green debris. Mrs. Blackstone carried the last of the metal buckets into the cooler and shut the light off. She pulled her blue cardigan around her as she pushed the door closed. She stamped her sturdy laced heels on the mat by the door.

The rest of the workers were smiling and whispering to one another. There were Walter and Henri. They were brothers whose family had immigrated from St. Emilie, Canada, just after World War II. They were always laughing as they worked. They had learned the rose business from William Blackstone. And now, there were none better than these two in all aspects of rose-growing, said Mr. Blackstone. Along with them were Mrs. Blackstone's brothers, Fred and Thomas Miller, who had partnered with their sister and brother-in-law to develop the Blackstone & Miller rose company.

Johnny, the delivery kid, was stacking the cardboard boxes from his last run of the day. He was Rickie's son. Rickie designed the arrangements, along with Mrs. Blackstone. She had started working there when she graduated from high school, learned the business, and been with them ever since. She set her last arrangement to the side. It was full of pink tea roses and baby's breath in a delicate white teacup.

Bradley Blackstone, the Blackstones' only child, was waiting, leaning against the counter with his hands stuffed in his leather jacket. He was a good-looking young man, although his looks were diminished by his arrogance. He seemed perturbed that he couldn't get to where he wanted to be. The workers all felt bad for the Blackstones. Bradley would never be part of the business. When he came into the shop, it was usually to ask his mother for money or give criticism of some sort to one of them. Even his mother was not immune to his barbs. Bradley went to Cornell University and, like Rose, was graduating next month. Rose was getting her degree in botany. He was in the School of Business but had no interest in his parents' business. He planned to work on Wall Street—"far away from this dirt," as he put it.

"Hey, Rose?" Bradley started with an almost haughty air.

"Yes, Bradley." Rose turned and forced a smile. Even though they all knew Bradley for what he was, he was still the boss's son, and so Rose remained pleasant.

"I got a job at Goldman Sachs in the city starting right after we get our diplomas. Are you still going to be getting your hands dirty? Do they still give degrees for that kind of stuff?"

While she wanted to comment on his egotistic conversation, Rose couldn't bring herself to answer.

"Rose, never mind Bradley. Come to the back. We have something to say to you." James Blackstone narrowed his eyes as he spoke to his son and then brightened as he turned his attention to Rose.

Bradley's smug expression quickly left his face. James was the only one that Bradley never dared to cross.

"Yes, sir, what is it?" Rose was unsure what was going on.

Mr. Blackstone's face was more stern than usual.

"Well, I'll get right to it. Since you'll be graduating in a few weeks, we wanted to make sure we, that is, we ah…" And just like that, the man in charge was at a loss for words.

"Oh, for heaven's sake, Jim," Madge Blackstone cut in. She shook her head as her husband began to stammer. "Rose, what Jim is trying to say is we're going to miss the living heck out of you. You've been such a constant here in the shop and in your work in the lab. We've just never had another student who has the love of this business at heart. We wish you the very best, and we have a couple of things for you." From under the counter, she brought out a small white corsage box tied with a red ribbon.

Jim stepped forward and placed a white letter-sized envelope next to it.

"I don't know what to say." Rose was blushing as she looked from kind face to kind face, ending with Bradley, who was almost sneering.

"Nothing to say, my petite one. Open them," Walter urged her with his heavy French accent.

Rose first undid the red satin ribbon and opened the box. Inside, pink tissue paper was fluffed up, creating a nest. As Rose reached into the fluff, she brought out a sterling silver rose on a handmade silver chain.

"Sadie over at the Silver Hammer made that for you," Madge explained.

She picked up the handcrafted necklace. The rose was a little larger than a silver dollar, and the detail of the petals was unbelievable. Rose put her hand to her mouth. "This is absolutely gorgeous."

Rickie came over and helped Rose fasten the clasp around her neck. Rose put her hand to it and shook her head. Next, she opened the envelope. She read the paper and held up a check.

"I don't understand," she said as she looked from Madge to Jim.

"We know you've been accepted in the master's program and that you'll most likely get a research job there. But we want you to stay, Rose. And if you can, we want you to work on developing the next varietals of hybrid roses. What do you say?" Jim had finally found his voice and smiled at her.

"I don't know what to say. I never imagined..." Rose's voice trailed off. She looked around at all of her "greenhouse family." The smiles on their faces made the decision for her. Her love of roses had begun when she walked through the cramped little shop and out into the greenhouses where the magic of roses began. The only face not smiling was Bradley, who stood with his arms folded across his chest and rolled his eyes. Rose opened the envelope, and inside was a note from James and Madge and a check for $5,000.

Acknowledgments

Through love and prudence, my parents, grandparents, sisters, extended family, and friends created my life pie with an environment rich in character and lessons. Some lessons seemed tedious at the time. The view from my rearview mirror of all those summer afternoons now sees these moments as some of the best times of my life.

Everyday life growing up in Canterbury, a rural town in Northeastern Connecticut, provided me with priceless memories. While I never journeyed too far from small-town USA, I found all types of individuals who filled my life with a variety of personalities and can be glimpsed within the stories and poems that you have just experienced. Life impacts you in layers of comings and goings, life and death. Some pieces of what you have read are reflections on the real times. Others, as in *The Summer of Strawberry Rhubarb Pie*, are those stories with rich characters within me that needed to come to life on the page.

My deepest thanks to Susanne Davis. From the moment we met, I asked her what she thought of my fishing newsletter. Her encouragement brings out the best in my writing. And my dear friend, Janet Jew, who never fails to help in those editing details.

To all of you who have accepted my writings into your hearts and homes, I am forever grateful. For those of you whom I have met in person, whether it be at a farmers market or a regional festival, I thank you for visiting with me and allowing me to share my love of writing with you. I hope all of you have enjoyed reading them as much as I have enjoyed writing them. And to my husband Eddy—who listens to each idea with patience, love, and encouragement—I have accomplished so many things with him by my side.

Please write to me at janedesrosiers51@gmail.com. Visit my website: www.janeherrdesrosiers.com.

The Summer of Strawberry Rhubarb Pie and my *Gone Fishing Trilogy* books are available from me, signed to whoever loves to read. They are also available on Amazon, Nook, Kindle, Apple iTunes Store, Google Play, and Barnes & Noble.

The novels of Jane Herr Desrosiers include *The Pincy Bluffs Trilogy, Gone Fishing: The Hook, Gone Fishing: The Line, Gone Fishing: The Sinker.*

Coming soon: *The Gardener, the Old Man, and the Cat.* Look for this book in the summer of 2024.

Books are available on Amazon, Nook, Kindle, Apple iTunes Store, Google Play, or Barnes & Noble.

Want your book signed by the author? Write to her at janedesrosiers51@gmail.com.

Follow her on Facebook, Jane Herr Desrosiers and Gonefishingthehook; on her website, http://www.janeherrdesrosiers.com; and on Instagram, @janeherr51.

About the Author

Jane Herr Desrosiers is excited to bring to her readers *The Summer of Strawberry Rhubarb Pie: A Collection of Stories and Poems from the Heart.* The response from readers of the *Gone Fishing* trilogy has reinforced her passion for writing. From her early days growing up in Canterbury, Connecticut, to her residence now in Baltic, Connecticut, her background provides the souls of her down-home characters. Retired from forty-five years in the healthcare information and risk management, she enjoys life with her husband, Eddy, and their family. She is a vice president of her town's library board that is a gem in her rural area of Connecticut. She enjoys public speaking about life experiences that have led her to becoming a writer. As she is fond of saying, "No one thought they would end up here today in this very spot." Contact her for a truly enjoyable experience for your next group meeting. For more information, you can visit http// www.janeherrdesrosiers.com as well as Facebook.com: Jane Herr Desrosiers, or email at janedesrosiers51@gmail.com.

www.ingramcontent.com/pod-product-compliance
Lightning Source LLC
Chambersburg PA
CBHW022049150726
47990CB00003B/1022